THE CHILD'S WORLD®

The Tale of Johnny Town-Mouse

Written by Beatrix Potter • Illustrated by Wendy Rasmussen

The Child's World

For Timothy and Grace

Published in the United States of America by The Child's World®
1980 Lookout Drive • Mankato, MN 56003-1705
800-599-READ • www.childsworld.com

ACKNOWLEDGMENTS
The Child's World®: Mary Berendes, Publishing Director
Editorial Directions, Inc.: E. Russell Primm, Editor; Dina Rubin, Proofreader
The Design Lab: Kathleen Petelinsek, Design; Victoria Stanley, Production Assistant

LIBRARY OF CONGRESS CATALOGING-IN-PUBLICATION DATA
Potter, Beatrix, 1866–1943.
  The tale of Johnny Town-Mouse / by Beatrix Potter ; illustrated by Wendy Rasmussen.
    p. cm. — (Classic tales)
  Summary: When the country mouse and the town mouse visit each other,
they discover they prefer very different ways of life.
  ISBN 978-1-60253-293-9 (library bound : alk. paper)
  [1. Fables. 2. Folklore.] I. Rasmussen, Wendy, 1952– ill. II. Aesop. III. Title.
IV. Series.
  PZ8.2.P57Tal 2009
  398.2—dc22 [E]   2009001634

The Tale of Johnny Town-Mouse

 ohnny Town-mouse was born in a cupboard. Timmy Willie was born in a garden. Timmy Willie was a little country mouse who went to town by mistake in a hamper. The gardener sent vegetables to town once a week by carrier; he packed them in a big wicker basket.

The gardener left the basket by the garden gate, so that the carrier could pick it up when he passed. Timmy Willie crept in through a hole in the basket, and after eating some peas, Timmy Willie fell fast asleep.

He awoke in a fright, while the basket was being lifted into the carrier's cart. Then there was a jolting and a clattering of horse's feet. Other packages were thrown in. For miles and miles—*jolt, jolt, jolt!*—and Timmy Willie trembled among the jumbled-up vegetables.

At last, the cart stopped at a house, where the basket was taken out, carried

in, and set down. The cook gave the
carrier a coin, the back door banged, and
the cart rumbled away. But there was no
quiet. There seemed to be hundreds of
carts passing. Dogs barked, boys whistled
in the street, the cook laughed, the parlor
maid ran up and down stairs, and a
canary sang like a steam engine.

Timmy Willie, who had lived all his life in a garden, was almost frightened to death. Presently, the cook opened the basket and began to unpack the vegetables. Out sprang the terrified Timmy Willie.

Up jumped the cook on a chair, exclaiming, "A mouse! A mouse! Call the cat! Fetch me the poker, Sarah!" Timmy Willie did not wait for Sarah with the poker. He rushed along the baseboard till he came to a little hole, and in he popped.

He dropped half a foot and crashed into the middle of a mouse dinner party, breaking three glasses. "Who in the world is this?" inquired Johnny Town-mouse. But after the first exclamation of surprise, he instantly recovered his manners.

With the greatest politeness, he introduced Timmy Willie to nine other mice, all with long tails and white neckties. Timmy Willie's own tail was insignificant. Johnny Town-mouse and

his friends noticed it, but they were too
polite to make personal remarks. Only
one of them asked Timmy Willie if he had
ever been in a trap.

The dinner was of eight courses, not
much of anything, but truly elegant.
All the dishes were unknown to Timmy
Willie, who would have been a little afraid
of tasting them. Only he was very hungry
and very anxious to behave with company

manners. The continual noise upstairs made him so nervous that he dropped a plate. "Never mind, they don't belong to us," said Johnny.

"Why don't those youngsters come back with the dessert?" It should be explained that two young mice, who were waiting on the others, went scouting around upstairs to the kitchen between courses. Several times, they had come tumbling in, squeaking and laughing. Timmy Willie learned with horror that they were being chased by the cat. His appetite failed. He felt faint. "Try some jelly?" said Johnny Town-mouse.

"No? Would you rather go to bed?
I will show you a most comfortable
sofa pillow."

The sofa pillow had a hole in it.
Johnny Town-mouse quite honestly
recommended it as the best bed, kept
exclusively for visitors. But the sofa
smelled of cat. Timmy Willie preferred to
spend a miserable night under the railing.

It was just the same the next day. An
excellent breakfast was provided—for
mice accustomed to eating bacon. But
Timmy Willie had been raised on roots
and salad. Johnny Town-mouse and his
friends noisily raced about under the

floors and came boldly out all over the
house in the evening. One particularly
loud crash had been caused by Sarah
tumbling downstairs with the tea tray.
There were crumbs and sugar and smears
of jam to be collected, in spite of the cat.

Timmy Willie longed to be at home
in his peaceful nest in a sunny bank.
The food disagreed with him. The noise
prevented him from sleeping. In a few
days, he grew so thin that Johnny Town-
mouse noticed it and questioned him.
He listened to Timmy Willie's story and
inquired about the garden. "It sounds
rather a dull place. What do you do when
it rains?"

"When it rains, I sit in my little
sandy burrow and shell corn and seeds
from my autumn store. I peep out at the
songbirds and blackbirds on the lawn and
my friend Cock Robin. And when the

sun comes out again, you should see my garden and the flowers—roses and pinks and pansies—no noise except the birds and bees and the lambs in the meadows."

"There goes that cat again!" exclaimed Johnny Town-mouse. When they had taken refuge in the coal cellar, he resumed the conversation. "I confess I am a little

disappointed. We have tried to entertain you, Timothy William."

"Oh, yes, yes, you have been most kind, but I do feel so ill," said Timmy Willie.

"It may be that your teeth and digestion are unaccustomed to our food. Perhaps it might be wiser for you to return in the basket."

"Oh? Oh!" cried Timmy Willie.

"Why of course for the matter of that we could have sent you back last week," said Johnny rather huffily. "Did you not know that the basket goes back empty on Saturdays?"

So Timmy Willie said good-bye to his new friends and hid in the basket with a crumb of cake and a withered cabbage leaf. And after much jolting, he was set down safely in his own garden.

Sometimes on Saturdays he went to look at the basket lying by the gate, but he knew better than to get in again. And nobody got out, though Johnny Town-mouse had half promised a visit.

The winter passed. The sun came out again. Timmy Willie sat by his burrow warming his little fur coat and sniffing the smell of violets and spring grass. He had nearly forgotten his visit to town.

When up the sandy path all fresh and clean with a brown leather bag came Johnny Town-mouse!

Timmy Willie received him with open arms. "You have come at the best of all the year. We will have herb pudding and sit in the sun."

"H'm'm! It is a little damp," said
Johnny Town-mouse, who was carrying
his tail under his arm, out of the mud.

"What is that fearful noise?" he
started violently.

"That?" said Timmy Willie. "That
is only a cow. I will beg a little milk.
They are quite harmless, unless they
happen to lie down upon you. How are
all our friends?"

Johnny's account was rather lackluster.
He explained why he was paying his
visit so early in the season. The family
had gone to the seaside for Easter. The
cook was doing spring-cleaning, on

board wages, with particular instructions
to clear out the mice. There were four
kittens, and the cat had killed the canary.

"They say we did it, but I know
better," said Johnny Town-mouse.
"Whatever is that fearful racket?"

"That is only the lawn mower. I
will fetch some of the grass clippings

presently to make your bed. I am
sure you had better settle in the
country, Johnny."

"H'm'm—we shall see by Tuesday
week. The basket is stopped while they
are at the seaside."

"I am sure you will never want to live
in town again," said Timmy Willie.

But he did. He went back in the very
next basket of vegetables. He said it was
too quiet!

One place suits one person. Another
place suits another person. For my part,
I prefer to live in the country, like
Timmy Willie.

ABOUT BEATRIX POTTER

When Beatrix Potter (1866–1943) was growing up in England, she did not go to a regular school. Instead, she stayed at home and was educated by a governess. Beatrix didn't have many playmates, other than her brother, but she had numerous pets, including birds, mice, lizards, and snakes. She enjoyed drawing her pets, and they later served as inspiration for her books.

As a young girl, Beatrix enjoyed going for walks in the country. She began drawing the animals and plants she saw. For several years, she also kept a secret journal, written in her own special code. The journal's code was not understood until after Beatrix died.

In 1893, when Potter was twenty-seven years old, she wrote a story for a little boy who was sick. That story became *The Tale of Peter Rabbit*. In 1902, the book was published and featured illustrations drawn by Potter herself. Her next book was *The Tale of Squirrel Nutkin*, which was published in 1903. Potter went on to write twenty-three books, all that were easy for children to read.

When Potter was in her forties, she bought a place called Hill Top Farm in England. She began breeding sheep and

became a respected farmer. She was concerned about the farmland and preserving natural places. When she died, Potter left all of her property, about 4,000 acres (1,600 hectares), to England's National Trust. This land is now part of the Lake District National Park. Today, the National Trust manages the Beatrix Potter Gallery, which displays her original book illustrations.

ABOUT WENDY RASMUSSEN

Drawing from the time she could hold her first crayon, Wendy Rasmussen grew up on a farm in southern New Jersey surrounded by the animals and things that often appear in her work. Rasmussen studied both biology and art in college. Today she illustrates children's books, as well as medical and natural-science books.

Today, Rasmussen lives in Bucks County, Pennsylvania, with her black Labrador Caley and her cat Josephine. When not in her studio, Rasmussen can usually be found somewhere in the garden or kayaking on the Delaware River.

OTHER WORKS BY BEATRIX POTTER

The Tale of Peter Rabbit (1902)

The Tale of Squirrel Nutkin (1903)

The Tailor of Gloucester (1903)

The Tale of Benjamin Bunny (1904)

The Tale of Two Bad Mice (1904)

The Tale of Mrs. Tiggy-Winkle (1905)

The Tale of the Pie and the Patty-Pan (1905)

The Tale of Mr. Jeremy Fisher (1906)

The Story of a Fierce Bad Rabbit (1906)

The Story of Miss Moppet (1906)

The Tale of Tom Kitten (1907)

The Tale of Jemima Puddle-Duck (1908)

The Tale of Samuel Whiskers or, The Roly-Poly Pudding (1908)

The Tale of the Flopsy Bunnies (1909)

The Tale of Ginger and Pickles (1909)

The Tale of Mrs. Tittlemouse (1910)

The Tale of Timmy Tiptoes (1911)

The Tale of Mr. Tod (1912)

The Tale of Pigling Bland (1913)

Appley Dapply's Nursery Rhymes (1917)

The Tale of Johnny Town-Mouse (1918)